AF414252

THE HUNGRY ALIEN
from
PLANET ZOG
DANDY AHAOMA
AHURUONYE

The Whispering Poet

DANDY AHAOMA AHURUONYE

THE HUNGRY ALIEN from PLANET ZOG

The universe is full of wonders, but only for those brave enough to explore it!

CREDITS

Illustrated by
dandyahuruonyebooks
Classic stories from the children's storyteller

INTRODUCTION

A Banquet for a Being from Beyond

This is a delightful cosmic adventure that will tickle your imagination and send your taste buds on a rocket-fuelled joyride. In a galaxy where meteor showers waltz and asteroids play hide-and-seek, Zog stands as a celestial hotspot—a place where laughter echoes across rainbow hills and moonflower vines bloom with dreams. But hold on to your space helmets, my star-hoppers, because something extraordinary is about to unfold. Brace yourselves for a meteoric invasion of humans! Yes, those peculiar creatures with wiggly noses and a fondness for mismatched socks. They arrived on Zog like a meteor storm crashing a lunar tea party. Their laughter bubbled like intergalactic soda pop, and their curiosity sparkled brighter than a comet's tail. Now, here's the cosmic twist: Zog had no police officers or soldiers. None whatsoever. Instead, they relied on the Alitool—a cloud of nanobots that floated like giggling jellyfish, scanning the cosmos for chuckles and chortles. These nanobots were Zog's secret guardians, keeping the peace with ticklish vibes and cosmic kindness. Imagine that—a universe where laughter is the ultimate superpower! Yes, here, laughter was the currency. And so, my little star-chasers, prepare for a tale that will make your antennae tingle and your imagination soar. It's a story of space sandwiches—yes, you heard right—sandwiches that break and mend with laughter. Of visa queues longer than comet tails (because even aliens need passports, as well as ask for passports). And of Constellation Cops wearing star-shaped badges, keeping Zog safe one giggle at a time.

But wait, there's more! Buckle up, cosmic adventurers, as we embark on a journey to Zog—the land where dreams twirl like shooting stars and even broken sandwiches find their way back together. Welcome to 'The Hungry Alien from Planet Zog.' Get ready to laugh, hug, and explore the universe, because on Zog, anything is possible—even a sandwich repair squad! Now, let's meet our hero: Dubal. He's not your run-of-the-mill Earthling. Oh, no! His freckles are constellations, and his unruly hair? Well, that's a nebula in the making. But Dubal has a hunger—a hunger that stretches beyond our blue planet's borders. He yearns for adventure, for a taste of the universe's secret recipes.

And then, one day, as he skips through dew-kissed grass, he stumbles upon a spaceship. But not just any spaceship! This one has more knobs, buttons, and gizmos than a grandma's knitting basket. And perched on top is an alien boy named Xain. Xain has four hands and three eyes that pop like overexcited popcorn. His voice? A cosmic symphony. "Greetings!" Xain says, "I'm from Planet Zog. We're famous for our intergalactic kebabs and disco-themed moons." Dubal's eyes widen. "Zog?" he echoes. "Sounds like a place where rainbows take vacations!" And so begins their friendship—a fusion of stardust and giggles. They cook up cosmic feasts in Dubal's kitchen, where the fridge hums ballads, and the sink moonlights as a water nymph. Xain marvels at the fiery dragon (a.k.a. the stove) and the frosty cavern (a.k.a. the fridge). But their hunger isn't just for earthly treats. Oh no! They dream of zipping through asteroid rings, sipping meteor showers, and discovering the ultimate spice—the elusive Galactic Garam Masala—Zog! With the construction of spacecrafts complete, they swiftly launch into space, leaving Earth in their wake, reminiscent of a curious neighbour observing from afar. Planet Zog welcomes them with open arms—or rather, with rainbow-furred aliens doing the cha-cha. The mayor, a three-eyed sage, awards them medals made of stardust. And the Alitool machine? It parks in the background, its gears humming a cosmic lullaby. "Welcome!" cry the aliens, waving banners in their squiggly language. "Try our Nebula Noodles and Meteor Muffins!" Dubal and

Xain dance through interplanetary food markets, juggling space veggies and sipping comet smoothies. The giant rings around Zog spin like hula hoops, and Earth sends a cosmic postcard: "Wish you were here!" If you follow them, you will discover what happened next. And if you manage to read the entire book, maybe you will get the opportunity to join them.

THE ZOGIAN POETRY

In the heart of the cosmos, far and wide,
    Lies a planet called Zog, where aliens reside.
With crystal mountains and oceans that glow,
It's a place of wonders, as far as planets go.
"Come explore Zog," the stars seem to say,
"Where every day is an extraordinary day.
From the break of dawn to the fall of night,
There's always something to bring delight."
On Zog, you see, there's no room for the mundane,
Every moment is unique, like a falling rain.
With an Alitool in hand and a heart full of zest,
Zogians create magic, they're simply the best.
They build floating houses, they grow glowing flowers,
They dance with the stars in the twilight hours.
They zoom through the sky in their flying cars,
Leaving a trail of stardust, like cosmic avatars.
"Come learn with us," the Zogians invite,
"Our Alischools are a scholar's delight.
From Alitot to Aliteen, we learn and we play,
Gaining new knowledge in a fun, exciting way."
On Zog, education is not a chore,
It's an adventure, a journey to explore.
With an Alitool as guide, and curiosity as the key,
The universe becomes a classroom, as vast as can be.
"Come play with us," the Zogian children call,
"In our games, there's a place for all.
From Galactic Goulash to Stellar crust,
We cook up fun in the most delightful way."

On Zog, play is not just about winning,
It's about creativity, it's about spinning
New ideas into games, into laughter and cheer,
Making memories that we hold dear.
So, pack your dreams, let your spirit take flight,
To Zog, where the stars shine bright.
For in this journey, you'll find, my friend,
That the universe is a poem, with no end.

PART TWO

Off to Zog, we take a leap,
In a spaceship, not too steep.
Through the stars and past the moon,
We'll be at Zog very soon!

"Look at that!" young Tim calls,
As a comet swiftly flies.
Galaxies twirl in a dance,
In this cosmic expanse.
Zog appears, a sight to see,
Full of aliens living free.
With their Alitools so bright,
Creating wonders day and night.
"Hello, Zogians!" we cheerfully greet,
Excited about the folks we'll meet.
They welcome us with a Zogian song,
In this place where we belong.
We learn about the stars above,
And the planets they all love.
Yorg and Vloorg, and Xezex too,
Each with a vista to pursue.
Back on Earth, we share our tale,
Of the planets, oh so frail.
We speak of Zog with a smile,
Wishing we could stay a while.
So, let's explore the cosmic sea,
For there's so much more to see.
Remember, space is a treasure trove,
Filled with wonders and stories to love.

GAMES OF ZOG: A TALE OF STARS & SKILLS

In the land of Zog, where the stars shine bright,
Alien children play, from morning till night.
They play Zogian games, under the golden suns,
Learning and laughing, having tons of fun.
***Zogian Zigzag**, a game of speed and grace,*
Teaches them teamwork, as they run the race.
With Alitools in hand, they zig and they zag,

Learning to lead, and when to lag.
***Galactic Goulash**, a game of wit and skill,*
Teaches them patience, and the power of will.
They stir and they mix, they taste and they twirl,
Creating a dish, that's out of this world.
***Stellar Soufflé**, a game of precision and art,*
Teaches them focus, and to play their part.
They whisk and they fold, they bake and they wait,
Learning that good things come to those who wait.

***COSMIC COCKTAIL**, a game of taste and flair,*
Teaches them creativity, and how to share.
They squeeze and they pour, they shake and they stir,
Learning that sharing brings joy, for sure.
Through these games, they learn so much more,
Values and skills, that open every door.
Teamwork and kindness, hard work and fun,
These are the lessons, under Zog's golden sun.
So here's to the children, of Zog and of Earth,
May they play and learn, and know their worth.
For in every game, in every playful bout,
It's the spirit of learning, that truly stands out.
So let's play and laugh, let's explore and roam,
In the vast universe, there's no place like home.
Whether on Earth or on Zog, under star or under tree,
We're all children of the cosmos, as free as can be

CHAPTER ONE

The Unexpected Encounter

Dubal was in the doldrums. His chums in the park had been engaged in the same old games for what felt like an eternity. Football, tag, hide and seek - it was all becoming a bit monotonous. Dubal craved something else; something different, an activity that would get his heart racing again. He yearned to venture into the uncharted territory of life and at that moment; he felt he would perhaps find some excitement in the forest that skirted the park, a place he had yet to explore. As his friends became engrossed in yet another round of their games, Dubal seized his chance and slipped away unnoticed, darting towards the trees with a sense of exhilaration. His mind buzzed with possibilities. What might he discover in the forest? Perhaps some exotic creatures, rare blooms, poisonous plants, or even hidden treasures. He hoped to find something so extraordinary that it would make his friends green with envy.

As he stepped into the forest, a sea of green enveloped him. The sounds of nature filled his ears - the birds' melodious song, the insects' rhythmic hum, the leaves whispering secrets to the passing sweet breeze. A cool wind caressed his face, carrying with it the scent of fresh earth. A smile spread across his face as he ventured deeper into the heart of the woods. He experienced wonder throughout his journey. He watched a cheeky and curious squirrel scamper up a tree, a butterfly performing its delicate dance, and a mushroom standing proudly on a log. As he wandered through the woods, a glimmer of hope sparked within him when he stumbled upon a sturdy stick. In his mind's eye, it transformed into a mighty sword, and he brandished it with all his might, creating a whooshing soundtrack to his adventurous tale. He felt like a gallant knight, ready to take on any challenge that lay ahead of him.

After a long journey, he came upon a radiant clearing bathed in the warm glow of the sun. In the centre of the clearing was a picturesque pond, its surface sparkling like a thousand diamonds, reflecting the sunlight in a mesmerising dance. The beauty of the scene took his breath away, and he couldn't help but pause to take it all in. A large rock, perfect for a rest, beckoned him. As he approached the rock, ready to take a well-deserved break, a strange noise reached his ears. He spun around, and his eyes widened in surprise. Standing before him was what looked like a boy, but unlike any he had ever seen. His skin was a vibrant iridescent blue, his hair a shocking purple, and his eyes a glowing yellow. As he observed the strange creature before him, the boy couldn't help but notice the details that made it so unique. Its ears were pointed, almost like an elf's, and twitched at every sound. Its long tail was incredibly flexible, swishing and curling behind it with ease. But what really caught his attention were its four arms, each one muscular and powerful. The creature wore an odd suit that seemed to be made of a combination of metal and wires, giving it a futuristic and high-tech appearance. A device attached to its wrist beeped and flashed with an urgent message, causing the creature to look down and assess the situation. It was clear that this being was not of this world, and the sight of it left the youngster in awe of what could exist beyond his immediate planet. He looked as scared and confused as the human boy felt.

Both of them stood still, rooted to the spot in shock, as they locked eyes with each other. The expression of bewilderment on their faces was palpable, and it was clear that they were both thinking the same thing: "What on earth is that?" Suddenly, their amazement turned into fear, and they both belted out blood-curdling screams that pierced the stillness of the surrounding woodland. Their screams were so thunderous that they startled the birds into flight, silenced the insects, and for a moment, even stilled the breeze. Even though they spoke different languages, the sheer terror in their screams allowed them to comprehend each other's fear. In that vast expanse, where the silence now reigned supreme, this sudden yelp pierced through the tranquillity. "Aaaah! An alien!" cried Dubal, his voice echoing through the atmosphere. The lad's shout was just as loud, "Aaaah! An Aliboy!" The two of them then fell silent; their faces reflecting a look of confusion and surprise. They had just realised that they had spoken the same words but with a slight variation. As they exchanged puzzled glances, their heads tilted, and brows furrowed, they were both trying to comprehend the strange situation they had found themselves in. The possibility of encountering an extraterrestrial being in the vast expanse of the universe had left them with a feeling of uncertainty and bewilderment. It was a moment of contemplation as they pondered the unknown, lost in their thoughts. "What's that you just said?" inquired Dubal, curiosity piqued. "And what might you have uttered?" echoed the boy, equally intrigued. Two young boys were engaged in a heated argument, their fingers pointed at each other in an accusatory manner. "You're an alien, a visitor from the vast void," Dubal declared, his voice filled with conviction. "No, you're the Aliboy, a chap from a different chapter," retorted the other boy, his tone equally assertive. Both shook their heads in denial, each convinced of their own point of view. "You're talking nonsense! I'm a human, a lad from this very locale," Dubal insisted vehemently. "Nonsense! You're the Aliboy. I hail from Zog, a young gent from my own sphere," countered the other boy with equal fervour. The argument continued to escalate with no end in sight."

CONFUSION REIGNED AS they endeavoured to explain.

"Behold, this is Earth. My abode, my patch, my little nook in the universe."

"And gaze upon Zog. My dwelling, my spot, my corner of the cosmos." They gestured skyward, presenting their respective worlds.

"Observe, yonder lies Earth. My origin, a sphere of blue and green hues."

"And behold, there's Zog. My genesis, an orb of purple and yellow shades." Eyes narrowed, they strained to glimpse the celestial specks. Each perceived a mere dot, a fleck in the firmament.

"I can't spot it. It's a stone's throw too far."

"I can't make it out. It's a tad too tiny." With a collective huff, they abandoned their celestial squabble.

"Let's not dilly-dally. Now tell me, how did you pop over here?" Dubal queried with a tilt of his head.

"Bit of a puzzler, that. I was frolicking with my Alipals in the green when a dazzling beam caught my eye. I toddled over, and voilà, here I am," Xain recounted with a shrug.

"That's very odd. I was equally at play with my mates in the park, when a murky silhouette beckoned. I trotted over, and there you were," Dubal told him, scratching his chin.

"A portal, perhaps? A thoroughfare through our worlds?" Xain pondered aloud.

"Could very well be. But the way back—how does one find it?" Dubal's brow furrowed deeper.

"Search for the portal again, we must," Xain suggested, eyes scanning the horizon. "Indeed, we must. But who knows its whereabouts?" Dubal echoed with hands on hips.

"A mystery it remains. Vanished, maybe? Concealed, likely?" Xain's shoulders slumped.

" Oh, my deadly! This is unfortunate. Home calls to us," Dubal sighed, a note of longing in his voice.

" Xain expressed his longing to return home and reunite with his loved ones, including his mother, father, siblings, grandparents, teacher, driver, pilot, and other important people in his life, with a tone tinged with sadness that conveyed the depth of his emotions.

"Wow, would you look at that! You've got quite an impressive entourage there. I can't help but wonder who might they be?" Dubal's eyes widened with curiosity.

"They're more than just acquaintances; all of them are family and friends, and some served as my mentors and companions, as well as my leaders and heroes," Xain explained proudly. "And I have a close-knit family, including a mother, father, sister, and brother. I have a close friend and roommate, a boss and a student, as well as a teacher and a driver. I'm even connected to a pilot and a monarch, a queen and a youngster," Dubal shared, echoing Xain's sentiment.

"We use different terms, but we are all alike," Xain noted, a smile forming on his face. "Although we differ in name, appearance, language, culture, and worldviews," Dubal agreed, his smile growing wider. "We are alike in our feelings, needs, aspirations, ambitions, and essence."

"Absolutely! We both love games, learning, and having fun," Xain said, nodding. "Perhaps we could be friends, helping each other find the portal," Dubal added, extending his hand.

"That's settled then. My name is Xain, by the way," Xain replied, shaking Dubal's hand firmly. "I'm Dubal. It's a pleasure to meet you, Xain," Dubal said, shaking Xain's hand with enthusiasm.

"Likewise, Dubal. I'm thrilled to meet you," Xain beamed.

As they clasped hands and exchanged grins, a sense of friendship kindled within them, accompanied by a glimmer of hope. With a united purpose in mind, they made a solemn vow to find the portal that would take them back to where they belonged. Despite the challenges ahead, they chose to embrace their predicament, to savour the thrill of their escapade, and to share a meal. Under the twinkling stars of Bumblebee town, they felt a surge of excitement for the new adventure that awaited them. As they gazed at the stars above, they couldn't help but feel excited about the adventure ahead. It would take them to Zog, a place of crystal mountains and glowing oceans, and would cement their friendship as truly out of this world. They both knew that their bond wasn't determined by where they came from, but by the shared memories they had created. With this in mind, they eagerly anticipated the new experiences and thrills waiting for them in both Earth and Zog.

CHAPTER TWO

Dubal and Xain's Unusual Adventure

The escapade began like this. Once upon a time, in a land where the grass whispered secrets and the trees high-fived passing birds, two intrepid explorers—Dubal and Xain—ventured forth. Their mission? To find the elusive galactic portal. But alas, their GPS had other plans, leading them in circles through the thick foliage. It was like Google Maps had taken a swig of fairy nectar and decided to play hide-and-seek. Dubal, with his unruly hair and a backpack full of snacks, was the eternal optimist. He believed that even a wrong turn could lead to a miracle bakery selling levitating doughnuts. Xain, on the other hand, was a realist. He'd brought a compass, a survival guide, and a frown that could scare off grumpy trolls. As they emerged from the lush maze, Dubal's eyes sparkled like dew-kissed dandelions. "Xain, we're on the brink of adventure! Imagine the tales we'll tell—of dragons, talking mushrooms, and Wi-Fi hotspots in ancient ruins."

Xain squinted at him. "Wi-Fi hotspots?"

"Yes! Imagine streaming spells on Netflix while sipping herbal tea with Merlin."

"But Merlin's not real," Xain protested.

Dubal winked. "Neither is my cousin's fashion sense, but we don't judge."

And so, as they trudged towards Dubal's home—a charming little cottage with a thatched roof and a gnome-shaped mailbox, Dubal's enthusiasm became contagious. "Xain, prepare your taste buds, because my mum's cooking can turn a broccoli into a disco ball."

Xain raised an eyebrow. "Disco broccoli?"

"Exactly! And my dad? He's the king of dad jokes. You'll be rolling on the floor, clutching your sides by the time he'd finished with you." Dubal said grinning. They kept walking until they reached the door, and Dubal flung it open.

For Xain, it was like arriving in a land where rejection tasted like overcooked Brussels sprouts and solidarity bloomed like dandelions in a sunbeam. The two unlikely companions—Dubal and Xain—found themselves shoulder to shoulder. They'd both been swiped left by the universe, but instead of wallowing in cosmic self-pity, they decided to form a club: "The Rejects Who Refuse to Sulk."

Dubal, with his unruly hair and a heart the size of a jumbo marshmallow, hesitated in front of the door before declaring, "Xain, we're in this together. We shall not retreat. Our parents may raise their eyebrows, but we'll stand our ground like stubborn garden gnomes." Xain adjusted his intergalactic spectacles he only wears when he feels a little cheeky. "Indeed, Dubal. We're comrades in arms now. And arms are handy for hugging. Let's embrace courage and hope like a warm, buttered crumpet; shall we?" And so, they knocked on the door of

Dubal's quaint cottage. The hinges groaned, and there stood Mum and Dad—Daisy and Danny—eyes wide as teacup saucers.

"Hey, everyone; I'm back! And I've brought a friend with me! Mum, Dad, meet Xain. He's from a distant realm. Arrived here by happenstance. Famished and weary. Needs our aid. But fear not, he's not a tax collector." Xain stepped inside, ready to meet Dubal's parents. He bowed, his antennae quivering. "Greetings. I apologise for any consternation. Your unfamiliarity with me is the sole culprit. Your kindness, like a perfectly steeped cuppa, is deeply appreciated." But their faces—oh, their faces—were a masterpiece of shock. They stared at him as if he'd just landed on their doorstep in a UFO-shaped teapot.

"Good heavens," they gasped. "What is that?"

Xain cleared his throat. "I'm Xain, not an alien. Although I do enjoy stargazing and occasionally abducting biscuits."

Dubal's parents exchanged glances. "An extraterrestrial in our own home!" they cried, bolting for the kitchen. The door slammed shut, muffling their frantic whispers. Dubal tugged at his hair. "Mum! Dad! He's not that kind of alien; he's an aliboy—a mate of mine!"

Xain chimed in, "Alimum! Alidad! Fear not! I'm Xain, and I'm his Alibuddy!"

From behind the barricade, the parental voices rose in a clamour. "Help! Help! Can anyone hear us? Help!!"

The boys huddled. "Perhaps we should depart," Xain mused. "They may not take kindly to me."

Dubal shook his head. "Or perhaps we should remain. They might require a moment. They might yet come around."

And so, they waited, like two lost satellites orbiting a cosmic kettle. Time ticked by, and finally, the kitchen door creaked slightly open and Dubal's parents peeked out, eyes wide. Seeing that the two lads huddled together and looking so calm, the parents began to relax, thinking, "Perhaps, it's not as bad as we thought!" The door then swung fully open, and they both emerged from the kitchen. Her first instinct was to be a hospitable host. So, she approached and spoke to the Aliboy.

"Xain," Dubal's mum said, "would you like a biscuit?"

Xain grinned. "Only if it's been abducted."

Dubal applauded enthusiastically. "Fantastic! We're now getting along like a house on fire. "I just wanted to take a moment to express my appreciation for you, Xain. Your exceptional qualities and character have made a significant impact on my life, and I value your presence more than words can express. To me, you're not just a friend, but more like family - someone I can always rely on and trust. I cherish our time together and the experiences we've shared so far, and I look forward to creating even more wonderful memories in the future. Thank you for being such a great companion, Xain.

Let's enjoy each other's company and have a fantastic time together." Laughter indeed erupted, swirling around the room like mischievous pixies. They resolved to deepen their acquaintance, exchange wisdom (Dubal's dad had a PhD in Dad Jokes), and revel in each other's company.

But the challenging part of their time together awaited: the alien feast. Dubal led the way to the kitchen, where pots and pans whispered secrets. "Xain," he said, "prepare your taste buds. We're about to concoct dishes that'll make your spaceship jealous." Hearing that, Xain's tail twitched as he adjusted his antennae. "Lead on, Dubal. I'm eager to sample your fare. Even if it involves pickled turnips or quinoa—things my home planet avoids like cosmic potholes." And so, they gathered—the humans, the alien, and the sentient spatula named Sir Whiskington. Dubal's sibling, Daisy chopped onions while Danny hummed a tune, and Xain tried not to sneeze into the pie crust before it was pushed into the oven. Within two minutes, Dubal's eyes sparkled because the pie was ready quicker than normal; might Xain have had something to do with it?

Anyway, Dubal pulled out the delicacy and announced, "Behold! The intergalactic shepherd's pie. It's like a hug from a nebula."

Xain took a cautious bite. "Not bad. A tad earthy. But I've had worse on Pluto."

Next came the cosmic crumpets, levitating slightly. "Spread with stardust jam," Dubal announced.

Xain grinned. "Tastes like meteor showers and childhood dreams."

As they feasted, the kitchen walls absorbed their laughter, becoming a mural of acceptance and oddball camaraderie.

And that, dear children, is how Dubal, Xain, and Sir Whiskington created the universe's first Intergalactic Chance Club. Their motto? "Weirdness is the spice of space." And so, they stirred, sprinkled, and shared—because even aliens need seconds. And that, dear children, is how Xain became the first aliboy in history to enjoy a cuppa and a meal with humans. As for the galactic portal? Well, it turned out to be a WhatsApp group chat for wizards. But that's another tale for another time.

CHAPTER THREE

The Kitchen Chronicles: A Culinary Conundrum

Xain had just had a meal on Earth with his human hosts, but the meal barely lasted an hour before he was hungry again and asked Dubal for another kitchen escapade. Dubal was very surprised and decided to bring him to the bigger kitchen where his mum prepared her restaurant meals. This cooking room was huge and had every kind of cooking utensils. Upon reaching the kitchen, Xain was met with a sight that left him utterly flabbergasted. His enormous eyeballs darted around, taking in the megastove, fridge, sink, table, and a myriad of other objects, each more baffling than the last. From the humble toaster to the mysterious microwave, from the simple spoon to the complex blender; to him, it was a veritable abundance of culinary contraptions.

"Zog vinegar! Do you earthlings need all this?" Xain exclaimed; his eyes wide with astonishment.

"Yep," replied Dubal's mum, with a hint of pride in her voice, "This is a modern, commercial kitchen, and we need everything you see here to whip up our contemporary cuisine."

"That's peculiar! Back on Zog, we prepare everything with just one device called the 'Alitool.' It seems humans have a fondness for showing off and clutter," Xain mused, shaking his head in disbelief. In the heart of this bustling kitchen, Dubal and his mum set about preparing a traditional Earth meal - spaghetti Bolognese. The tantalising aroma of the simmering sauce wafted through the house, making everyone's mouth water. However, when they served the meal to Xain, he looked at it with a puzzled expression.

"NOW, JUST HEAR ME OUT, please. Yes, I know I shared that initial meal with you; I did that so as not to come across as rude. But that's not how I usually eat. In Zog, we don't eat at a table. We absorb nutrients from our surroundings," Xain explained.

Dubal and his parents were taken aback, but they didn't want to make Xain uncomfortable. "Well, Xain, here on Earth, we sit at the table and eat our meals. Would you like to give it a try again?" Dubal asked. Xain hesitated for a moment, then nodded. "I'll give it a whirl," he said. And so, they all sat down at the table, a human family and an Aliboy, sharing a meal and a moment that they would remember for the rest of their lives. But as Xain took his first mouthful, his face turned a shade of green. It was clear that he didn't find the meal to his liking. Dubal and his parents exchanged glances, wondering what they could do to make Xain feel more at home. As the sunset and the stars began to twinkle in the sky, Dubal made a promise to himself. He would find a meal that Xain would enjoy, no matter how many tries it took. And with that thought, he looked forward to the adventures that inevitably awaited them.

CHAPTER FOUR

Wow; aliens eat a lot!

In the heart of their culinary escapade, Dubal and Xain danced through the kitchen like sugar-fuelled ogres. Their mission? To explore the rainbow of ingredients and create a dish that would make taste buds do the conga. Laughter bubbled like a mischievous potion, and the air hummed with the scent of adventure. Dubal, with his apron tied like a superhero cape, declared, "Xain, my intergalactic amigo, behold our arsenal! We've got knives, forks, spoons, and enough gadgets to launch a spaceship to Zog." Xain's antennae quivered with excitement. "Dubal, my old mate, let's wield these tools like wizards. I've always wanted to slice and dice like a cosmic ninja." And so, they embarked on their culinary quest. First up: peeling. Dubal demonstrated, carrot in hand. "Xain, my carrot-crunching comrade, watch closely. A peeler is like a wonder wand. Swipe it gently, and voilà! Naked carrots." Xain mimicked the move, eyes wide. "By the moons of Jupiter! It's like undressing a veggie. I feel positively regal."

Next, grating. Dubal handed Xain the grater. "Imagine this as a cheese-surfing board. Grate the cheese like you're shredding stardust off a giant crag." Xain grinned. "Cheese-surfing? I'm in! Weee! Look over here, Dubal, it's snowing cheddar!"

Whisking came next. Dubal whisked eggs like a whirlwind. "Xain, my cosmic egg whisperer, beat those eggs till they froth like meteor showers." Xain twirled the whisk. "Frothy eggs? I'm ready for liftoff! Houston, we have an omelette."

Stirring, boiling, baking—they conquered them all. Dubal's cookbook floated like a spellbook, revealing crusts full of secrets. Xain's timer beeped like a starship alarm, ensuring nothing burned to a crisp. And then it was time for the chicken and rice casserole. Dubal sprinkled salt like a seasoning sorcerer. "Salt, my salty sidekick, elevate our creation. Make it sing like a cosmic choir and take me home!" Xain tossed in parsley, leaves fluttering like green confetti. "Parsley, my leafy legend, dance with the carrots and eggs. We're creating a blend of flavours."

The kitchen table transformed into a banquet hall. Dubal set places; napkins neatly folded. Xain arranged coasters, each one a mini planet.

And there, at the head of the table, sat their guest—an alien with four hands, three eyes and a fork. Dubal was ecstatic. "Greetings, extraterrestrial friend! Join us in our gastronomic odyssey. Our chicken and rice casserole awaits." The Zogian hesitated, then took a bite. Its eyes widened. "By the quasars! This is nectar! The carrots sing, the eggs moonwalk, and the parsley waltzes. Ambrosia indeed! I love it. Let's call it 'Galactic Goulash.'"

And so, they feasted—like a team of adventurers, united by food and laughter. As stars winked outside the window, Dubal whispered, "Xain, my friend, we've cooked up more than a meal. We've cooked up memories." And Xain, with crumbs on his antennae, replied, "Yes, dude; memories seasoned with laughter are the best kind."

No one knew aliens had an insatiable appetite. Xain just wants more and more food and Dubal had to spend most of his time in the kitchen so as not to displease his new pal. So, once again, Dubal and Xain embarked on a new culinary adventure. Dubal, with his apron tied around his waist and a chef's hat perched on his head, looked every bit the part of a master chef. Xain, on the other hand, looked slightly out of place with his green skin and starry eyes, but his enthusiasm was infectious all the same.

"Xain, today we're going to make something a little different – a traditional Earth dish called Shepherd's Pie. It's a hearty meal made with minced meat and vegetables, and topped with mashed potatoes." Xain looked intrigued. "That sounds interesting, Dubal. But remember, on Zog, we absorb nutrients from our surroundings. I've never eaten anything like this before; are you sure I would like this meal?" Dubal nodded, understanding Xain's apprehension. "Don't worry, Xain. We'll take it one step at a time." And so, they began. Just as he did before, Dubal showed Xain how to peel and chop the vegetables, how to cook the meat until it was brown and crumbly, and how to mash the potatoes until they were fluffy and light. Xain watched in awe, fascinated by the process; as if it was his first. He had evidently forgotten the previous lesson. As the Shepherd's Pie baked in the oven, the kitchen filled with a delicious aroma. Dubal and Xain set the table, anticipation building with each passing minute. After what felt like a couple of minutes, the oven timer beeped; the meal was ready. Dubal carefully took the dish out of the oven, the golden-brown crust of the pie steaming and inviting. He served a portion to Xain, who looked at it with a mixture of curiosity and apprehension.

"Go on, Xain. Give it a try," Dubal encouraged.

Xain picked up his fork and took a small bite. He chewed slowly; his expression unreadable. Dubal held his breath, waiting for Xain's verdict.

Finally, Xain swallowed and looked at Dubal. "It's... different from the previous bake, but not bad. I think I could get used to this."

Dubal let out a sigh of relief. "I'm glad you liked it, Xain. And don't worry, there are plenty more Earth dishes for you to try."

Afterwards, the boys remained at the table, sharing stories and laughter. It was a moment neither of them would ever forget - the start of an extraordinary friendship and the first of many meals shared together. And so, under the twinkling stars and the soft glow of the kitchen light, Dubal and Xain's culinary journey continued, promising more adventures, more laughter, and more unforgettable meals. And that, dear children, is how Dubal, Xain, and an alien from Zog created the tastiest tale in the entire universe.

CHAPTER FIVE

Dubal and Xain's Cosmic Cook-Off: A Recipe for Friendship

In a kitchen that was situated in a place that seemed incredibly distant (well, actually, it was Dubal's mum's kitchen), a story began with the timeless phrase "Once upon a time." That day, two culinary adventurers—Dubal and Xain—donned their aprons and set forth on another grand cooking odyssey. Their mission? Their mission was to embark on a journey to discover the incredible edible treasures of Earth and craft culinary creations that would make taste buds dance in joyful celebration.

Pancakes: Dubal introduced Xain to the joy of fluffy pancakes. "Behold, the golden discs of delight! Topped with maple syrup—a liquid hug from trees—and a sprinkle of fresh berries, they're like edible rainbows."

Xain's antennae shuddered. "Fluffy pancakes? I'm in! But why flip them? Are they secretly acrobats?"

"Exactly! Pancakes are the Cirque du Soleil of breakfast meals. They flip to impress the syrup."

Pizza: One sunny afternoon, Dubal and Xain transformed the kitchen into a pizza battleground. They kneaded dough like warriors preparing for battle. "Tomato sauce," Dubal announced, "is our secret weapon. And cheese—oh, Xain, brace yourself—it's like a dairy disco in your mouth."

Xain's eyes widened. "Cheese? A food item that didn't exist on Zog! It's like a moon crater of deliciousness."

Vegetable Stir-fry: Dubal, determined to introduce Xain to veggies, wielded a rainbow of peppers, carrots, and broccoli. "Xain," he said, brandishing a wok, "this is our vegetable canvas. Chop, stir, and behold the colours!"

Xain sliced veggies with gusto. "By the cosmic quarks! It's like Picasso meets stir-fry. I see red in the middle, green on the outskirts, and a hint of intergalactic purple all over. Oh, my deadly!"

Spaghetti Carbonara: Dubal's favourite pasta dish was next. He twisted spaghetti around his fork like a pasta wizard. He couldn't contain his enthusiasm as he explained, "Dude, you won't believe it, but this mouthwatering dish right here is none other than Spaghetti Carbonara. It's like a creamy hug from an Italian grandma; the only difference being that she was running during the hug."

Xain slurped. "Creamy? I'm floating on a cloud of Parmesan dreams."

Apple Pie: For dessert, Dubal taught Xain the ancient art of apple pie. "Xain," he said, flour dusting his nose, "This crust is our buttery fortress. And inside? Sweet, tangy apples. It's like a hug from autumn."

Xain tasted. "By the quasars! It's like biting into a warm hug. And the buttery crust? I want to build a spaceship out of it right now."

And so, through sizzling pans and flour storms, Dubal and Xain not only cooked up deliciousness but also shared stories. Xain regaled Dubal with tales of Zog's floating marshmallow mountains, while Dubal described Earth's moon landings and disco cheese parties. Their friendship blossomed like a well-risen crust. And as they sat down to feast, Xain raised his fork and expressed his appreciation, "Thank you for the lessons, the pancakes, pizza, veggies, pasta, and pie!" Dubal responded, "You are welcome; I wish us a stronger friendship—a recipe that transcends galaxies." And that, my little cosmic chefs, is how Dubal and Xain created more than meals. They cooked up memories, sprinkled with laughter and seasoned with stardust.

ALITOOL

CHAPTER SIX

The Marvellous Mysteries of Zog

In a far-off corner of the cosmos, there exists a world that is a spectacle to behold. This world, known as Zog, is the celestial abode of our young Aliboy, Xain. Picture, if you will, a realm where the heavens blush a radiant shade of lavender, and the leafy grass twinkles like a sea of emeralds under the watchful gaze of three golden suns. This, dear reader, is the enchanting spectacle that is Zog. Zog's environment is as varied as a painter's palette. Majestic mountains, composed entirely of crystal, tower over the landscape, their surfaces dancing with iridescent light. Oceans, vast and deep, teeming with bioluminescent creatures, casting an unusual glow across the water's surface. Forests, dense and lush, are home to trees that bear fruit in every hue you could possibly imagine. The air is a symphony of sweet, fresh fragrances, punctuated by the gentle hum of Zog's unique fauna. The inhabitants of Zog, or 'Aliens' as we Earthlings might call them, have cultivated a society that is both technologically advanced and harmoniously balanced with nature. Their dwellings, constructed with an eco-conscious design, blend seamlessly into the landscape. Craftsmen use a remarkable device known as the 'Alitool' to create these homes.

The Alitool, a testament to Alien ingenuity, is a multi-functional marvel. This device can metamorphose into any tool or machine its user requires. Constructing a dwelling? The Alitool can shape-shift into a hammer, a saw, or even a crane. Crafting a vehicle? The Alitool can transform into a wrench, a screwdriver, or a welding torch. It's the Swiss Army knife of Alien technology, making life on Zog both efficient and sustainable. Despite their technological prowess, the Aliens lead lives of simplicity. Their days are spent exploring the breathtaking beauty of their planet, gaining knowledge about the universe, and creating art that mirrors their experiences. They hold in high regard the virtues of knowledge, creativity, simplicity, and harmony with nature.

"Back on Zog," Xain told Dubal, "we don't have many institutions of learning like you do on Earth. Instead, we gain knowledge by exploring our world and the cosmos beyond. Our Alteachers guide us, but they don't administer many tests or assign endless grades. They believe that the joy of learning is reward enough." His tales of life on Zog captivated Dubal.

He envisioned the crystal mountains, the taste of the animated fruits, and the experience of using an Alitool. He yearned to visit Zog and witness its wonders firsthand. And as Xain told him stories, a seed of a dream took root in his heart. He didn't know the 'how' or the 'when', but he was certain that one day, he would journey to Zog and behold the alien world with his own eyes. For the time being, however, he was content with his newfound friend and the adventures they embarked upon on Earth. After all, who needed to voyage to an alien planet when he had an Aliboy right here in Bumblebee town?

The Alitool Amazement

NESTLED IN THE HEART of Zog, amidst the shimmering crystal mountains and the luminescent oceans, lay the secret to the advanced and harmonious life of all the Aliens - the Alitool. This remarkable piece of technology was the cornerstone of Alien society, a tool so versatile and efficient that it had revolutionised the way the Aliens lived. One day, Xain took it upon himself to explain the marvel of the Alitool to Dubal. "Imagine having a mate who can transform into anything you need, Dubal. That's what the Alitool is for us," Xain had said, his eyes twinkling like distant galaxies. The Alitool, a small, handheld device, was no bigger than a pebble. Its smooth, round surface emitted a soft, iridescent glow. But its size was deceiving. This tiny device held within it the power to transform into any tool or machine an Alien could ever need.

But how did the Alitool work? As Xain explained, the user's thoughts powered the Alitool. "You just have to imagine what you need, and the Alitool transforms into it. It feels like magic, right? But it's not. It's science," Xain said, a note of awe in his voice. The Alitool was more than just an instrument; it was a symbol of the Aliens' philosophy of life. They believed in living in harmony with their environment, and in being resourceful and efficient. The Alitool embodied these values, enabling the Aliens to build and create while preserving the natural beauty of Zog. As Dubal listened to his stories about the Alitool, he couldn't help but marvel at the advanced technology of Zog. He imagined what it would be like to have an

Alitool of his own, to be able to create anything he needed with just a thought.

And so, under the twinkling stars of Bumblebee town, Dubal dreamed of Zog and its wonders, of Aliboys and Alitools, and of a friendship that spanned galaxies. His dreams were full of laughter, adventure, and the promise of many more exciting days to come.

CHAPTER SEVEN

The I-Explorer Games

Dubal and Xain, despite hailing from different corners of the universe, found a shared love for adventure and learning. One activity that they particularly relished was exploring the park - the very place where their paths had first crossed. This park, with its towering trees and bustling insect life, had become their favourite haunt. They would spend hours on end, delving into every nook and cranny of the park. From the tallest trees that seemed to touch the sky to the smallest insects scurrying in the undergrowth, nothing escaped their curious eyes. They experienced the joy of discovery and shared experiences throughout their days.

One of their favourite games was I-Explorer. In this game, Xain would describe a creature or plant from Zog, and Dubal would try to find something similar in the park. "It's like a game of intergalactic I-Spy," Dubal would say, his eyes sparkling with excitement. "Alright, Dubal," Xain would start, "I'm thinking of a Zogian Flutterbug. It's small, has six legs, and wings that shimmer in the sunlight." Dubal would then scour the park, looking for an Earthly equivalent. More often than not, he'd return with a beaming smile and a butterfly gently resting on his finger. "A butterfly!" he'd exclaim. "It's small, has six legs, and wings that shimmer in the sunlight. Just like your Flutterbug!"

Their conversations were a delightful mix of Earthly and Alien topics. They discussed everything from the complexities of interstellar travel to the simple pleasure of kicking a football. They shared stories and jokes and even made up their own silly songs. "Two friends from two worlds, having a jolly good time," Dubal would often sing, with Xain joining in the laughter. As the sun set, painting the sky with hues of orange and pink, they would often lie on the grass, looking up at the twinkling stars. "That one's Zog," Xain would point out, "and that's Earth," Dubal would add. Despite the millions of miles between their homes, in those moments, it felt like they were just a stone's throw away.

The other activity that they loved was cooking new dishes. After their first culinary adventure, they continued to explore Earth cuisine with gusto.

They would spend some afternoons in the kitchen, trying out new recipes, laughing at their culinary mishaps, and learning from them to improve their skills. One of their successful creations was the Galactic Goulash, a hearty chicken and rice casserole with stew on the side that combined the earthy flavours of Dubal's world with the exotic spices of

Zog. It was a hit, not just with Dubal and Xain, but also with Dubal's parents, who praised the boys for their culinary creativity.

Then there was the Stellar Crust Pie, a dessert that was as light as a cloud and as sweet as the nectar from Zog's moonflowers. It was a delicate dance of flavours that left everyone asking for seconds, and wondering, "Where on Zog did you find this recipe?" And who could forget the Cosmic Cocktail, a drink that sparkled like the night sky and tasted like a burst of interstellar joy? It was a concoction of Earth's ripest fruits and Zog's sweetest nectars, a drink truly worthy of a planetary celebration. Yes, whenever they cooked together, there was always a delightful mix of amusement and just the right amount of chaos. They had fun in every moment, engaging in playful flour fights and dealing with accidental sauce splatters, as well as the occasional burnt toast mishap. Dubal would often break out into his usual song, "Two friends from two worlds, creating a universe of flavours," and Xain would join in on the sing-along.... As they cooked, it was clear that they both loved trying new things, and they both believed that food tasted better when shared with a friend.

Another activity that Dubal and Xain particularly relished was stargazing. On clear nights, they would lie on the grass, their eyes tracing the paths of distant celestial bodies. Xain would point out the constellations of Zog, while Dubal would share stories about the constellations of Earth. The constellation that Xain often pointed out was the Zogian Zephyr, a group of stars that, to the Aliens of Zog, resembled a swift, cosmic wind. Another was the Galactic Giggler, an assemblage that seemed to twinkle in a pattern that reminded the Zogians of laughter.

Dubal, on the other hand, would talk about The Great British Lion, a constellation that resembled a majestic lion, and The Jester's Hat, a group of stars that looked like a jester's cap, complete with bells that seemed to jingle in the night sky. They would also discuss the various stars, moons, and galaxies they could see. Xain introduced

Dubal to Zog's Beacon, the brightest star in the Zogian sky, and The Laughing Luna, Zog's native moon that, according to Alien folklore, chuckled at its own reflection in the resplendent Zogian seas. Dubal, in turn, would point out Earth's own celestial wonders. He showed Xain The North Star, Earth's reliable guide, and The Moon, our planet's loyal companion. He also shared stories about The Milky Way, our home galaxy that looked like a brushstroke of spilt milk across the night sky.

Their stargazing sessions were not just about observing the stars, but also about sharing their cultures, their myths, and their marvels. They would lie side by side, their laughter and whispers floating up to the twinkling stars above. As they traced the paths of shooting stars and satellites, they would share stories and jokes, their laughter piercing through the starlit sky. "Two friends from two worlds, under a blanket of stars," Dubal often sang, with Xain joining in; oh, the Zogian sang so well, and these stargazing sessions became a cherished ritual for both boys. As they gazed up at the vast cosmos, they were reminded of how vast the universe was, and how fortunate they were to have found a friend in each other.

They found it thought-provoking that, despite the vast expanse of space that separated their respective homelands, these were moments that felt as though they were mere neighbours, just a stone's throw away from one another. The indescribable bond between them transcended the physical distance that separated them, making it feel as though they were always in the same room, sharing the same air and experiencing the same emotions. These moments were rare and fleeting, but they left a lasting impression that would linger long after they had gone their separate ways. Through these adventures, Dubal and Xain didn't just explore the park; they explored friendship, understanding, and the joy of discovering new things together. Their story was a testament to the fact that no matter how different we might seem, at the end of the day, we all share the same universal love for happiness, knowledge, and a good adventure.

CHAPTER EIGHT

Teaching Playful Games to the Alien

Dubal and Xain were involved in other pastimes. One day, Dubal introduced Xain to some of Earth's popular games like football, hide and seek, and tag. He, in turn, taught Dubal some of the games that Aliens play on Zog. The next game that Dubal introduced was Earthly Echo, a game where one person would shout a word, and the other would have to find an object that rhymed with it. "Tree!" Dubal would shout, and Xain would run to find a bee buzzing around a flower. The game was filled with fun and silly rhymes, and it quickly became a favourite for the boys.

Xain, on the other hand, introduced a game from Zog called Zogian Zigzag. In this game, one player would create a zigzag pattern in the air with their finger, and the other player would have to replicate it exactly. "It's all about memory, attentiveness and agility," Xain would say, his many arms moving in a blur as he created complex patterns for Dubal to follow. They would spend hours playing these games, each trying to outdo the other. There was friendly competition, but also a lot of fun. "Two friends from two worlds, playing games under the sun," Dubal would often sing, with Xain joining in the duet.

Xain's tales about Zog fascinated Dubal. The Zogian Zephyr and the Galactic Giggler particularly intrigued him. His curiosity about Xain's culture and way of life made Xain feel accepted and valued. On the other hand, Xain was equally curious about Earth. He enjoyed learning about its customs and traditions from Dubal, especially the games like Earthly Echo and the Coral Castles under Earth's seas. Their shared love for adventure also strengthened their bond. They were both curious and open-minded, qualities that helped them embrace their differences and learn from each other. They respected each other's opinions and always listened with an open mind. Over time, their bond grew stronger. They learned to communicate effectively, understand each other's emotions, and support each other in times of need. And despite coming from worlds far apart, they found common ground and built a friendship based on mutual respect, understanding, and shared experiences. Their story is a beautiful example of how friendship can transcend boundaries and bring together individuals from different backgrounds.

It shows that with understanding, respect, and a shared sense of adventure, a human boy and an alien can become the best of friends. Their friendship is a testament to the power of connection and the universal language of friendship.

As they journeyed further and further through their adventures, they created a myriad of memories. From the laughter-filled cooking sessions to the quiet moments of stargazing, each memory was a testament to their unique friendship. And as they looked forward to more adventures, they knew that they had a friend in each other, a friend who would be there through thick and thin, a friend who understood them, and a friend who shared their love for adventure. And to them; that was the most beautiful adventure of all. Yes, the boys didn't just have fun; they also learned about each other's cultures and ways of thinking. They discovered that true friendship knows no boundaries, not even those of different worlds.

CHAPTER NINE

Xain is Homeward Bound

Dubal and Xain, despite hailing from different corners of the universe, found a shared love for adventure and learning. Their friendship, forged through shared experiences and mutual respect for each other's differences, had grown stronger with each passing day. However, as the days turned into weeks, and the weeks into months, Xain began to feel a tug in his heart. It was a feeling he couldn't quite put into words, a longing for the familiar sights and sounds of Zog. He missed the sparkling crystal mountains, the glowing oceans, and the gentle hum of Zog's unique wildlife. He missed his Alimum and Alidad, his Alipals, and the comfort of his own world. Xain was homesick.

As a result, one starlit night, as they were lying on the grass, gazing at the cosmos, Xain turned to Dubal. "Dubal," he began, his voice barely above a whisper, "I'm not sure how to put this delicately enough, but I miss Zog." Dubal looked at Xain, his heart aching for his friend. "I can't even begin to imagine how hard it must be for you, my friend. But remember, you always have a home here with us." Xain smiled, grateful for Dubal's words. But there was something else he needed to say. "Dubal," he said, "I've been thinking... I want to go back to Zog." Dubal was silent for a moment, processing Xain's words. He knew this day would come, but it still took him by surprise. "I understand, Xain," he finally said. "And I want you to know that I support your decision." Xain looked relieved, but there was a hint of sadness in his eyes. "Thank you, Dubal. That means a lot to me. But there's one more thing..." Dubal waited, sensing that Xain had something important to say. "Would you... would you like to come to Zog with me?" Dubal was taken aback. He had never considered the possibility of visiting Zog. But the more he thought about it, the more excited he became. "Xain, I would love to visit Zog with you," he said, his eyes shining with anticipation. With that, both of them agreed on the date for their escapade to Zog. Xain planned to use an Alitool in his pocket to make the trip possible by building two small crafts that will carry each one of them.

And so, under the twinkling stars of Bumblebee town, a new adventure was about to begin. An adventure that would take them to Zog, to crystal mountains and glowing oceans, and to a friendship that was truly out of this world. As they lay there, looking up at the stars, they knew that their friendship was not defined by where they came from, but by the memories they had created together. And with that thought, they looked forward to the adventures that awaited them in Zog.

CHAPTER TEN

The Zogian Zeal: A Voyage to Zog

The day of departure had finally dawned. Dubal and Xain stood at the edge of Bumblebee town, their hearts aflutter with a cocktail of excitement and apprehension. They were on the precipice of an adventure that would whisk them across galaxies and plunge them into the unknown realms of Zog. As they activated their Alitools, transforming them into spacecrafts, Dubal turned to Xain. "Are you ready, Xain?" he asked, his voice barely above a whisper. Xain nodded, his starry eyes reflecting the twinkling stars above. "I am, Dubal. Are you?" Dubal took a deep breath, his grip tightening around the handlebars of his Alitool. "I am," he said, his voice filled with determination. And so, they set off, their spacecrafts soaring into the night sky, leaving behind the familiar sights of Bumblebee town.

As they travelled through space, they marvelled at the beauty of the universe, the twinkling stars, and the vast emptiness that stretched out before them. Their journey, however, was not without challenges. Halfway through their voyage, Dubal's Alitool started to flicker. "Xain," Dubal called out, his voice filled with worry, "my Alitool... it seems to be running out of power; do you think we'll make it to Zog?" Xain looked at Dubal, his eyes wide with concern. "Hold on, mate. I'm coming. Somehow, we have to keep going because Zog awaits us, with its crystal mountains and bioluminescent oceans. We can't turn back now." With a swift movement, Xain manoeuvred his spacecraft towards Dubal. He extended a tow line from his Alitool, attaching it to Dubal's spacecraft. "Don't worry, pal; I've got you," Xain said in a steady and reassuring voice. With Xain's Alitool towing him, they continued their journey. It was a tense and silent ride, the only sound being the hum of their Alitools. But despite the fear and uncertainty, Dubal felt a sense of calm. He knew he wasn't alone. He had Xain by his side.

As they approached the outer edges of the Zogian atmosphere, the colours shifted from indigo to violet. The three golden suns cast elongated shadows on the landscape below. Dubal's heart raced as he steered his towed spacecraft toward the planet's surface, following closely behind Xain; his eyes wide with wonder. They descended through the lavender-hued clouds, and suddenly, there it was—the enchanting world of Zog.

The crystal mountains sparkled like giant diamonds, and the forests whispered secrets to the passing breeze. Xain's arms trembled with the excitement of coming home. But after they'd been travelling quietly for a while, Dubal broke the silence, "Xain, this is more magnificent than I ever imagined!" Xain grinned. "You haven't seen anything yet! Hold on, pal. We're about to land." Thus, after what felt like a lifetime, the brilliant lights appeared closer and closer; yes, it was Zog, its three golden suns shining brightly against the backdrop of space. As they approached the planet, Dubal couldn't help but marvel at its beauty. It was unlike anything he had ever seen or imagined.

As soon as their spacecrafts touched down on a grassy knoll, they quickly stepped out onto Zogian soil, and Dubal turned to Xain, his eyes filled with gratitude. "We made it, Xain. Thank you, my friend." Xain smiled, "Yes, we made it; we made it. Welcome to Zog! But we're not home yet; we still have to chart our route to my town on the other side of the planet." The air smelled of sweet nectar, and the leaves rustled in greeting. A group of Zogian creatures, resembling a cross between squirrels and fireflies, flitted around them. "Welcome, Earthlings!" one creature chirped. "I am Glitterwing. How may we assist you?" Dubal bowed. "Glitterwing, we seek the galactic portal that will take us home. Can you guide us?" Glitterwing's antennae twitched. "Ah, the portal! It lies beyond the Crystal Caves, guarded by the Wise Crystals. But beware—the path is treacherous." Xain adjusted his intergalactic flying spectacles. "Treacherous, you say? Sounds like my kind of adventure."

And so, after repairing Dubal's machine, Xain and Dubal set off, their Alitools now at the ready. They traversed the crystal-studded mountains, crossed the bioluminescent oceans, and encountered talking mushrooms that offered riddles. The Wise Crystals awaited them in the heart of the Crystal Caves, their luminous faces ancient and kind. "You seek the portal to travel home; we've been informed. Is that so?" they intoned. "Well, we've got news for you! To open it, you must dance the Zogian Shuffle." Xain and Dubal exchanged glances. "The Zogian Shuffle?" Dubal asked. Xain wiggled his four arms. "Don't you worry, pal; I've been practicing. We can do it. Let me show you how to do the dance!"

And so, under the watchful gaze of the Wise Crystals, Dubal and Xain shuffled, twirled, and spun. The ground trembled, and a vortex appeared—a swirling gateway to the far side of the Zog world where

Xain and his family live. "Step through," the Wise Crystals said. "Zog will always welcome those who dance with joy." Xain took Dubal's hand. "Ready?" Dubal grinned. "Absolutely." And hand in hand, they stepped into the portal, leaving behind the crystal mountains and the talking mushrooms. Zog's vortex pulled them in and then embraced them, its lavender skies and emerald grass a testament to the wonders of the cosmos. Soon, they arrived at Xain's part of Zog, and, wow! Was the boy glad to come home? And so began Dubal's grand adventure on Zog, albeit with Xain's help and guidance—a tale of friendship, courage, and the sheer wonder of dancing your way to the stars. The Hungry Alien from Planet Zog was home and ready to help Dubal explore every nook and cranny of this extraordinary world.

And so, under the golden Zogian suns, a new chapter in their friendship began. A chapter filled with fresh adventures, new experiences, and the promise of many more to come. As they stood there, looking up at the alien sky, they looked forward to the adventures that awaited them in Zog.

CHAPTER ELEVEN

The First Human on Planet Zog

In the vast expanse of the cosmos, our protagonist, Dubal, found himself in a whirlwind of emotions as he encountered an array of extraterrestrial beings. His heart pounded with curiosity, his mind buzzed with excitement, his palms sweated with nervousness, and his spine tingled with fear. The enigma of the alien world intrigued him, sparking a thirst for knowledge about these interstellar inhabitants. The prospect of embarking on an unprecedented journey and making friends from galaxies far away thrilled his adventurous spirit. Yet, the pressure to leave a positive imprint on these beings and steer clear of any potential mishaps made him jittery. The fear of the unknown, the unfamiliar, and the distinctly different sent shivers down his spine.

Dubal pondered over the extraterrestrials' perception of him, their treatment towards him, and their intentions. He harboured hopes of encountering amicable beings, not those harbouring hostility. He wished for assistance, not adversity; for amusement, not monotony. In the back of his mind, he also harboured a peculiar hope - that he would not end up as an alien's dinner! The extraterrestrials, on their part, had varied reactions to Dubal. A group of them, led by an alien named Laya, exhibited curiosity. They yearned to unravel the mysteries of Dubal and his terrestrial home. They actively absorbed his responses, engaging him in conversation, and reciprocated by sharing glimpses of their culture and language. Their friendliness was palpable, and they welcomed him with open arms, although the thought of him as a potential meal did cross their minds!

However, not all shared this sentiment. Fear gripped Xain's parents, for instance. The sight of Dubal and his makeshift Alitool sent shockwaves through them. They perceived him as a potential threat, choosing to maintain a safe distance and cautioning him to also keep his distance, refraining from causing any disruption. Their fear led them to reject him outright, and they certainly did not consider him as a potential meal. Xain's rival, Laya, who seemed positive about Dubal earlier, changed his stance and was now seething with anger. Jealousy gnawed at him as he saw Dubal's growing friendship with Xain.

Suspecting Dubal to be a spy, he sought to unmask him. He challenged Dubal to a duel, hoping to emerge victorious. His hostility towards Dubal was evident, and yet, he harboured no intentions of having Dubal as a meal. Xain's sister found Dubal's antics amusing. She found his mannerisms hilarious and often burst into laughter at his expense. She playfully teased him with jokes, thoroughly enjoying his company. She liked Dubal, and the thought of him as a potential meal did bring a smile to her face!

Lastly, there were those like Xain's Alteacher who remained indifferent. Engrossed in their own lives, they paid little heed to Dubal. They considered him irrelevant and chose to focus on their work instead. They neither liked nor disliked him, simply tolerating his presence. Thus, Dubal's interstellar adventure was filled with a mix of emotions, encounters, and experiences, making for a truly out-of-this-world tale! And remember, no matter how tasty Dubal might have seemed, he was definitely not on the Zogian menu!

CHAPTER TWELVE

The Captivating Planet

In a far-off galaxy, on the enchanting planet of Zog, two unlikely companions, Dubal and Xain, embarked on a series of extraordinary escapades. Their journey was a kaleidoscope of adventures, each more thrilling than the last. They traversed the shimmering crystal mountains, their peaks piercing the indigo skies. They plunged into the radiant oceans, their waters aglow with bioluminescent life. They even indulged in a quaint picnic, basking in the glow of the tri-solar sunset, a spectacle that painted the sky with hues of orange, pink, and gold. Xain, the native of Zog, took it upon himself to acquaint Dubal with the local flora and fauna, a vibrant array of life forms that could alter their colours at will or serenade them with harmonious tunes. The creatures were a mix of colour and sound, a testament to the planet's rich biodiversity. Their adventures also led them to an Alien gathering, a grand assembly of the Zog inhabitants. Here, Dubal was introduced to the planet's unique societal structure. The females were called Aligirls, the mothers were known as Alimums, and the fathers were referred to as Alidads. Even the adolescents had a special moniker - Aliteens. This encounter with the Alien society left Dubal utterly fascinated. The harmonious coexistence, the respect for nature, and the advanced technology, particularly the Alitool, captivated him. He marvelled at how the Aliens utilised the Alitool, a device that seamlessly blended creation with conservation, preserving the natural beauty of Zog. As for the bond between Dubal and Xain, it flourished amidst these adventures. Dubal's admiration for Xain amplified as he observed Xain's seamless adaptation to his home environment and the respect he commanded among his fellow Aliens. Xain, in turn, appreciated Dubal's open-mindedness and eagerness to immerse himself in a new culture. Their shared experiences on Zog served to strengthen their bond, helping them navigate their differences and cherish their unique friendship.

In conclusion, their journey was a tale that tickled the imagination, a testament to the power of friendship, and a reminder that the universe is full of wonders waiting to be discovered. So, dear children, let this tale inspire you to dream, explore, and cherish the bonds of friendship. Remember, the universe is a playground, and you are its adventurers. Happy exploring!

CHAPTER THIRTEEN

The Grand Farewell and the Homeward Journey to Earth

As the sun set on the alien planet of Zog, the moment had arrived for young Dubal to bid adieu and embark on his journey back to his terrestrial abode. His sojourn on Zog had been an extraordinary collection of adventures, from scaling the shimmering crystal mountains to diving into the luminescent oceans, and most significantly, nurturing a deep bond of friendship with the Zogian, Xain. On his ultimate day, he found himself amidst Xain and his kin, his heart burdened with the melancholy of parting. "I shall miss you all dearly," Dubal expressed, his voice quivering with emotion. "We shall miss you too, Dubal," Xain's Alimum, who didn't like him at the beginning, responded, her eyes now brimming with affection. "If you ever changed your mind, you shall always find a home here on Zog." Xain's Alidad advanced, cradling a small, radiant object in his hand. It was similar to the Alitool Dubal had used, but it had its own distinctive features; emanating a steady, iridescent glow, and pulsating with an unseen energy. "Dubal," Xain's Alidad initiated, "this is a unique Alitool. We have customised it for your voyage back to Earth. It shall never exhaust its fuel." Their kind consideration deeply moved Dubal. "Thank you," he responded, accepting the Alitool. "I shall cherish this." Following that, Xain guided Dubal to a quiet and isolated location, where he proceeded to showcase the operation and features of the innovative Alitool. He explained the controls, the safety protocols, and the method of refuelling it using cosmic energy if he ever needed it.

Dubal paid heed, rehearsing until he was confident of his mastery over the powerful machine. And soon, the hour of departure dawned. The boy ascended into his spacecraft, his heart throbbing with a cocktail of exhilaration and apprehension. He cast a last glance at Xain and his family, engraving their appearances in his memory. "Goodbye, my friends," Dubal voiced, his words reverberating in the tranquil expanse of Zog. "Safe travels, Dubal," Xain reciprocated, his starry eyes glistening with unshed tears. "Remember, you shall always have a home here on Zog." With a concluding wave, Dubal activated his engine. The spacecraft ascended, piercing the star-studded sky. As Zog diminished in the distance, Dubal charted his course for Earth. The homeward journey was extensive, but Dubal was not solitary.

He had the Alitool, a symbol of his extraordinary camaraderie with Xain, and the memories of his incredible escapade on Zog. As he approached Earth, a sense of wonder overwhelmed Dubal. The adventurer was a lad from the humble Bumblebee town, but now returning from an extraterrestrial planet, bearing tales of crystal mountains, glowing oceans, and a friendship that transcended galaxies.

Beneath the vibrant azure sky of Earth, a new chapter unfolded in Dubal's life, as the air whispered with the gentle rustling of leaves and the sweet scent of blooming flowers embraced his senses. A chapter of disseminating his experiences, treasuring his friendship with Xain, and envisioning his subsequent adventure.

CHAPTER FOURTEEN

The Zogian Chronicles: Adventures with the Alitool

An exclusive energy source powered the Alitool, an extraordinary piece of engineering from the Zogian civilization, called Zogite. This mineral, extracted solely from Planet Zog by the Zogian civilization, was a rare and valuable resource. The use of Zogite in the Alitool allowed it to perform remarkable feats that were previously unimaginable. The Alitool could transform this energy into various forms, enabling it to create a multitude of tools and utensils. One day, the innovative Zogian scientists started a mission to build a groundbreaking new tool, using the exceptional capabilities of the Alitool. They named it the Healotron. The process of creating the Healotron was meticulous and fascinating. First, the Zogians inputted the design specifications into the Alitool. Then, the Alitool used its Zogite power to materialise the Healotron. Inspired by the success of the Healotron, they embarked on a series of ambitious projects, each more innovative than the last. The Alitool, with its transformative Zogite power, was at the heart of these endeavours. The first of these was the NutriMaker, a device capable of synthesising nutritious food from simple elements. The Zogians programmed the Alitool with the molecular structure of various foods. The Alitool then used its Zogite power to rearrange atoms into these structures, creating a feast from glowing water and thin air! Next came the EduProjector, a learning tool that could project holographic images and lessons. The Zogians designed this tool to make learning fun and interactive. The Alitool used its Zogite power to generate the holograms, bringing the lessons to life. The engineers didn't stop there. They also created the TeleTraveller, a device that could transport them instantly to any location on Zog. The Alitool, powered by Zogite, manipulated the fabric of space-time to achieve this remarkable feat. These inventions revolutionised life for ordinary citizens. The NutriMaker solved food shortages; the EduProjector made learning very exciting, and the TeleTraveller eliminated the need for vehicles, reducing pollution. Every Zogian believed that sharing their technology with other civilisations could bring about universal prosperity. After Dubal's successful visit, they envisioned humans visiting Zog, learning from their advancements, and using this knowledge to combat diseases prevalent on Earth.

The Healotron, for instance, could revolutionise healthcare. It could manipulate cellular structures, potentially curing diseases like cancer and heart disease. The NutriMaker could provide nutritious food, combating malnutrition and high blood pressure. The EduProjector could enhance education, leading to breakthroughs in medical and scientific research.

CHAPTER FIFTEEN

Alitools and Zogian Education

In the far reaches of the cosmos, nestled amidst the twinkling stars and swirling galaxies, lies the planet of Zog. Home to a unique species of aliens, Zog is a world filled with wonders and marvels that would boggle the human mind. But perhaps the most fascinating aspect of Zogian life is their education system, a system that revolves around a remarkable device known as the Alitool. The Alitool, a small, handheld device, is the cornerstone of Zogian society. This versatile tool can transform into any object or machine an alien could ever need, making it an essential part of everyday life on Zog. From building houses to cooking meals, the Alitool is used in every aspect of Zogian life. But mastering the Alitool is no easy feat. It requires skill, precision, and a deep understanding of Zogian science. And that's where the Zogian education system comes in.

On Zog, education begins soon after birth because the aliens are born with in-built intelligence. In the world of Zog, the young ones, known as Alitots, are initiated into the realm of learning as soon as they are able to hold an Alitool. Alischools, which are specialised educational institutions, have been created with the purpose of providing Alitots with the necessary knowledge and skills to effectively and responsibly utilise their Alitools. Through these schools, the Alitots gain the skills and training necessary to wield their Alitools effectively and with great responsibility.

The curriculum at an Alischool is diverse and comprehensive. Alitots learn about the science behind the Alitool, including the principles of transformation and the laws of Zogian physics. They also learn practical skills, such as how to transform their Alitool into different objects and machines. As Alitots grow older, they progress to higher levels of education. They attend Aliteen schools, where they learn more advanced Alitool techniques and delve deeper into Zogian science. They also begin to specialise in certain areas, such as Alitool engineering, Alitool programming, how to programme the transformative Zogite power, as well as Alitool design. After graduating from Aliteen school, Zogians have the option to attend university or Aliuni. At Aliuni, they can further specialise in their chosen field and conduct research to advance Zogian science and Alitool technology.

The Zogian education system is not just about academic achievement. It's also about personal growth and community development. Zogians believe that by mastering the Alitool, they can contribute to their society and lead fulfilling lives. Moreover, their education system encourages creativity and innovation. Zogians are always finding new ways to use their Alitools, leading to exciting discoveries and advancements. This culture of innovation is a key reason why Zog is considered one of the most advanced civilisations in the cosmos.

But was there an opportunity there for earthlings? Absolutely! For humans, a journey to Zog could be an opportunity to learn about a different way of life. By observing the Zogians and their education system, we could gain insights into new methods of teaching and learning. Humans could also learn about sustainable living, as the Zogians use their Alitools to meet their needs without needing too much technology that is very expensive and could ruin the environment. Yes, theirs was a diverse and interconnected world.

The Zogian Qualifications: The Zogian education system also offers a unique set of qualifications. The Zogian education system awards Alidents a 'Star of Mastery' in their chosen field upon completion of their studies. These stars, which are actually miniature Alitools, serve as a testament to the Alident's skill and expertise. The more stars an Alident has, the more respected they are in their field. For example, the 'Star of Invention' may be awarded to an Alident who has mastered the art of Alitool engineering, while the 'Star of Codes' may be given to one who excels in Alitool programming, and 'Star of mechanics' to an Alident who excelled in Alitool upgrades, servicing and repairs. On Zog, the Alidents held these qualifications in high regard and they take great pride in them.

CHAPTER SIXTEEN

The Journey to Zog: A Leap of Faith

A journey for any human to Zog would undoubtedly be a leap of faith that would require courage, curiosity, and an open mind. But for those willing to take the plunge, the rewards could be immense. Imagine being able to study in an Alischool, learning about the Alitool and the wonders of Zogian science. Imagine exploring the glowing, animated gardens, floating forests, and crystal mountains of Zog. Imagine meeting Aliboys and Aligirls, learning about their games and culture, and making Alipals. And most importantly, imagine the knowledge and perspective you would gain. The understanding that there are countless ways to live, learn, and grow. So, to all the young explorers out there, we say this: Dare to dream. Dare to explore. Dare to take the journey to Zog. Who knows? You might just find that the simple, sustainable lifestyle of the Zogians is not just possible, but desirable. And in the process, you might just discover a whole new way of looking at our own world.

After all, as the Zogian saying goes, "The universe is full of wonders for those who are brave enough to explore." So why not start your exploration today?

In the distant reaches of the cosmos, nestled within the swirling nebulae and radiant star clusters, there exists the beautiful galaxy of Zog. Within this celestial wonderland, a young alien named Xain resided. Unlike the typical inhabitants of his kind, Xain was a vibrant and energetic lad, brimming with an insatiable thirst for adventure.

His friends would often call out to him during their cosmic football matches, "Xain, it's your turn to kick the ball!" With a swift and powerful kick, Xain would send the ball hurtling across the interstellar expanse, leaving a trail of stardust in its wake. Xain's sister was a courageous girl named Galaxia, who was always prepared to embark on any space adventure that came her way. "Brace yourself, universe! Galaxia is on her way!" she would announce, her voice reverberating through the galaxies. She was a spectacle to behold, spinning under the twinkling stars, her movements as captivating as the trail of a shooting star. The pillars of this extraordinary alien neighbourhood were Alimums and Alidads. An Alimum, the nurturing alien mother, ensured that all her little aliens were well-nourished and prepared for their interstellar journeys.

"Alimum, what's on the menu tonight? Are we having Zogspaghetti?" Xain would inquire, his eyes sparkling with anticipation. Alidad, the sagacious alien father, would navigate his family through the cosmos, recounting tales about the stars that left his children in awe. Aliteen, the adolescent alien, was constantly striving to fit in at their intergalactic school. Despite often feeling like an outsider, he embraced his uniqueness, proudly identifying himself as an Aliteen.

Alitot, the endearing toddler of the family, was learning to navigate the zero-gravity environment. "Just look at that Alitot, floating around like a tiny asteroid butterfloat!" the Alimum would exclaim, watching her youngest with a sense of pride as he learns the art of movement.

The term Alibling was used to refer to an alien sibling. Xain and Galaxia, being Aliblings, would explore new planets together, sharing countless adventures. Alipal was a term used to denote a friend, and Xain and Galaxia had many Alipals at their intergalactic school. They were not just friends, but also Alimates, sharing their classroom and numerous exhilarating experiences. Their Alivisor at school was a wise and patient alien who guided them through their lessons. "Our Alivisor assigned us an exciting project today!" Xain would exclaim, eager to acquire new knowledge. As Alidents, they were always ready to learn, preparing for their intergalactic exams under the guidance of their Alteacher. The term Aldriver was used to refer to their school bus driver, who navigated through traffic with ease. "Our Aldriver ensured our safe arrival at school today," Galaxia would say, expressing gratitude for the smooth journey. And when they played with their toy cars, Xain would proudly declare, "I'm the Aldriver of this lunar rover." The leader of their team was the Aliking, the ruler of the alien crew. "Our Aliking devised a brilliant plan for our mission," Xain would say, admiring their leader's strategic acumen. And when the leader was a female, she was the Alienqueen, and this term was also used for the queen of the cosmos.

And so, life in Zog was filled with fun, learning, and lots of adventures. Every day was a new journey, a new story, and a new opportunity to create memories that would last a lifetime. And though they were extraterrestrials, their lives were not so different from ours. After all, whether on Earth or in Zog, the joy of family, friendship, and discovery is universal. So, the next time you look up at the stars, remember Xain, Galaxia, and their wonderful alien world. Who knows, you might just spot them playing a game of intergalactic football under the cosmic lights.

CHAPTER SEVENTEEN

The Alitool Transforms Everything Else

We're now fascinated by the cornerstone of Zogian innovation: the Alitool. This compact, handheld device, no larger than the smallest star in the Zogian sky, holds the power to metamorphose into any object or machine that a Zogian could ever require. But one might wonder, how does this miraculous transformation process function? The Alitool operates on a principle that is as fascinating as the cosmos itself - the principle of matter manipulation. It employs the most advanced Zogian technology to rearrange the atoms and molecules of its own structure, morphing seamlessly into the object desired by its user. This process is controlled not by buttons or switches, but by the user's thoughts, which are picked up by the Alitool's highly sensitive thought receptors, as delicate and precise as the orbits of the planets. For instance, if a Zogian wishes to transform their Alitool into a hammer, they simply have to visualise the hammer, large or small, in their mind. The Alitool, with its thought receptors as sensitive as a butterfly's wings, picks up on this mental image and commences the transformation process. Within mere seconds, faster than a comet streaking across the night sky, the Alitool reshapes itself into a hammer, ready for use.

But the Alitool's capabilities do not end there. It's not just a tool for the extraordinary, but also for the ordinary. Even the most common Zogian resident, from the youngest to the oldest, can use the Alitool to create other tools, regardless of their type. Need a spoon to stir your soup? Then just visualise it, and the Alitool transforms. Need a telescope to gaze at the distant stars? Picture it in your mind, and the Alitool becomes one. The Alitool, consequently, is not merely a device; it is a companion, a helper, and a testament to the limitless potential of Zogian technology. It's a tool that has shaped the lives of the Zogians, making the impossible possible and turning dreams into reality. So, the next time you look up at the stars and wonder about life in the far-off galaxy of Zog, remember the Alitool, the marvel of Zogian innovation that makes the extraordinary ordinary.

CHAPTER EIGHTEEN

How They Celebrated Achievements on Zog

In a far-flung galaxy where the stars twinkle like a child's eyes full of wonder, residents celebrated achievements with an enthusiasm as boundless as the universe itself. Whether it's the mastery of a new transformation using the remarkable Alitool, or the joyous occasion of graduating from an esteemed Aliuni, every accomplishment, no matter how big or small, is recognised and applauded with heartfelt sincerity. One of the most popular and cherished ways to celebrate these milestones is through the grand Starlight Ceremony. This ceremony is as magnificent as the cosmos itself, filled with the soft glow of interstellar lights and the harmonious molecular melodies; the organisers played these tunes by using the Alitool to record some of the sweetest melodies from every corner of the universe, and playing them back to the attendees. During this awe-inspiring ceremony, the achiever receives a Star of Excellence, a miniature Alitool that glows with a soft, iridescent light, just as mesmerising as a distant nebula. The Star of Excellence is not just a symbol, but a testament to the achiever's relentless hard work, unwavering dedication, and indomitable spirit; making it a source of immense pride, a beacon that shines brightly, illuminating the path for others to follow.

The Starlight Ceremony is a grand event, a spectacle that transcends the ordinary. All the Zogians attended it, their hearts filled with joy and their eyes sparkling with anticipation. The air is filled with the melodious strains of music, the infectious sound of laughter, and the tantalising aroma of Zog's finest delicacies. It's a time for everybody to come together as one, to celebrate the achievements of their fellow Zogians, and to bask in the shared joy of accomplishment. Yet, the festivities on Zog encompass more than just the Starlight Ceremony. Throughout the year, the Zogians participate in a myriad of social events and festivities. Each event is a vibrant show of tradition, innovation, and camaraderie. From the Galactic Games, where they showcase their athletic prowess, to the Cosmic Carnival, a festival of art, culture, and cuisine, there's always a reason to celebrate on Zog.

Preparing for these grand celebrations is a community effort. Everyone, from the youngest to the oldest, contributes in their own unique way.

Some lend their artistic skills to create stunning decorations, while others use their culinary talents to prepare a feast of intergalactic delicacies. The Alitool plays a crucial role in these preparations, transforming into whatever tool is needed to get the job done. Funding these grand celebrations is a testament to the Zogians' sense of community and shared responsibility. Every Zogian contributes according to their means, creating a communal fund that ensures every celebration is a success. Whether it's contributing Alicoins, offering their skills and services, or donating resources, every contribution is valued and appreciated.

And so, life on Zog is a continuous celebration of achievements and shared joy. Every day brings new challenges to overcome, new milestones to achieve, and new reasons to have fun. So, the next time you gaze at the stars, spare a thought for the Zogians, celebrating their achievements under the cosmic lights.

CHAPTER NINETEEN

Exploring the Cosmos' Many Other Planets

In the boundless expanse of the cosmos, where stars twinkle like diamonds strewn across a velvet blanket, lies the intriguing planet of Zog. This celestial body, with its unique inhabitants and advanced technology, is indeed a marvel to behold. However, Zog is not a solitary entity in its galaxy. A myriad of other planets accompanied it, each with its own mysteries and wonders, all waiting to be discovered. Adjacent to Zog, at a distance that could be traversed in a few Zogian light years, lies the planet of Yorg. Yorg, much like Zog, is a gas giant, its atmosphere composed primarily of helium and hydrogen. However, unlike Zog, Yorg's landscape is a mesmerising array of floating islands, suspended in the planet's dense atmosphere. These islands, made of a unique, buoyant mineral found only on Yorg, are home to a variety of exotic flora and fauna. The Yorgians, as the inhabitants are known, have adapted to live in this unique environment, their bodies altered to float effortlessly between the islands.

A little further away from Zog, nestled in the comforting warmth of a nearby star, is the rocky planet of Vloorg. Vloorg's surface is a rugged terrain of towering mountains and deep canyons, carved over millennia by the planet's fierce winds. Despite its harsh landscape, Vloorg is teeming with life. The Vloorgians, resilient and hardy, have developed the ability to withstand the planet's extreme weather conditions. They live in elaborate cave systems, their lives intertwined with the rhythm of their planet.

Closer to Zog, orbiting the same star, is the water world of Xezex; a planet covered entirely in a vast, global ocean. Beneath its tranquil waves lies a vibrant underwater world, illuminated by shapeless creatures that call it home. The Xezetians are an aquatic species, their bodies streamlined for swift movement through the water. They live in sprawling underwater cities, their architecture a harmonious blend of technology and nature.

Despite the differences in their landscapes, atmospheres, and inhabitants, these planets share a common trait with Zog - they are all teeming with life. Each planet, with its unique ecosystem and diverse species, contributes to the rich mixture of life in the galaxy.

Exploring these planets is no small feat, and requires careful planning, advanced technology, and a spirit of adventure. The Zogians, with their Alitools and interstellar ships, are well-equipped for this task. They embark on these explorations with a sense of curiosity and wonder, eager to learn more about their cosmic neighbours. Funding these explorations is a communal effort. Every Zogian contributes according to their means, creating a communal fund that ensures every exploration mission is a success. Whether it's contributing Zogian

Alicoins, offering their skills and services, or simply donating resources, every input is valued and appreciated.

The cosmos never fails to captivate their imagination. With each new planet they explore and every new species they discover, their understanding of the universe grows, fuelling their endless fascination with the mysteries of the cosmos. As they traverse the vast expanse of the cosmos, their hearts brim with an insatiable curiosity and an unquenchable thirst for knowledge. Driven by an unyielding desire to unravel the enigmas of the universe, they bravely venture forth, navigating through the infinite reaches of space with a sense of wonder and awe.

CHAPTER TWENTY

Zog's Alitool: The Galactic Guardians of Peace

Once upon a time, in the twinkling expanse of the Zogian cosmos, there existed a planet like no other—a place where alien laughter echoed across rolling hills that hung upon nothing, and the skies shimmered with interstellar confetti. But here's the twist: Zog had no police officers or soldiers. None; Nada, Zilch! You see, Zogians were a quirky bunch. They wore hats made of gold dust and shoes that squeaked like cosmic rubber ducks. But uniforms? Nah! They preferred glittery capes and feathered boas. So, when it came to law and order, they had a different trick up their three sleeves—Ah; you guessed it; the Alitool. They weren't gadgets or spaceships; nope. They were super-smart clouds made up of nanobots that floated above Zog like a celestial jellyfish. Their mission? To keep the peace, maintain harmony, and prevent cosmic chaos. How? Let's dive in:

The Whispering Breeze – The gadget had a hotline to every Zogian's brain. When someone even thought about mischief, it sent a gentle whisper: "Hey there! I know that moon rock looks tempting, but maybe we should think twice before taking it. It's important to respect and preserve scientific artefacts for the benefit of everyone. What do you think?" Zogians called it the "Nudge of Niceness."

The Hug-o-Meter – The Alitool measured hugs per hour. Seriously. If you hugged your neighbour, the Alitool gave you a star sticker. Zogians loved stickers. They stuck them on their antennae and giggled.

The Giggle Detector – Laughter was the Alitool's secret weapon. It floated through Zog's parks, tickling kids and grown-ups alike. "Giggle more, grumble less," it advised.

The Cosmic Compassion Quotient – The Alitool scanned hearts. If yours glowed with kindness, you got a virtual high-five. "Kindness is cooler than comet surfing," it reminded everyone. Now, in all this, there were The Great Zogian Benefits:

Peaceful Picnics – They picnicked under rainbow trees, sharing space sandwiches and asteroid juice. No fights. Just giggles and crumbs.

Space Traffic Jams? Nah! – The Alitool directed cosmic traffic. No honking. No road rages. "Patience, my starlings; even the comets tire out!" it said.

The Budget Boon – No police stations. No jails. No uniforms; thus, they saved lots of starbucks (the currency, not the coffee).

Galactic Gratitude – Zogians used to show gratitude to the Alitool at bedtime; this made the Alitool to blush (yes, it could blush).... But after Xain returned from Earth, he educated them about an Almighty designer and creator called Jehovah, and with that their eyes opened and they now gave thanks to this Supreme being "Thanks Jehovah for all you've given us, and the peaceful dreams," they whispered before nodding off.

The Alitool didn't need a badge or a laser gun. It just needed love, laughter, and a sprinkle of gold dust. As the Zogian saying went: "When in doubt, just hug it out!"

And that, my little cosmic adventurers, is how Zog stayed safe, sparkly, and splendid. But now you might be wondering a little about the Giggle Detector, Zog's Cosmic Chuckle Guardian. So, let's talk more about it. It began at a time when asteroids moonwalked and meteor showers threw glitter parties. That was when this marvellous invention—the Giggle Detector came into existence. Now, you might wonder, "What on Zog is a Giggle Detector, and why do those Zog need one?" Buckle up little stardust sprites, as we unveil the cosmic secrets of this giggle-powered wonder. Long ago, when Zogians still wore socks on their antennae (don't ask), the Galactic Council faced a dilemma. How could they maintain peace and order without stern-faced officers or grumpy space soldiers? Enter the Giggle Detector—a cloud of nanobots that floated like giggling jellyfish, scanning the cosmos for chuckles and chortles.

In the heart of Zog's Techno-Garden (where daisies hummed binary code), lived Professor Quirk. With his rainbow lab coat and a hat shaped like a quasar, he invented things that made the stars jealous. One day, while sipping asteroid tea, he had an epiphany: "Why not harness laughter to keep Zog safe?" The Giggle Detector had sensors sharper than comet tails. It listened for giggles, snickers, and belly laughs. "Laughter is our cosmic currency," Professor Quirk declared. Then there was the Giggle Grading. When Zogians laughed, the Giggle Detector graded them. A hearty guffaw earned five stars; a polite chuckle got three, and a simple smile received one star. "Giggle responsibly," Professor Quirk reminded everyone. This invention also led to the Anti-Grump Shields. The Giggle Detector emitted invisible waves that repelled grumpiness. If someone scowled, it zapped them with ticklish vibes (no, not electric shocks). "No frowns allowed," the prof insisted.

At this point, I might as well tell you about The Great Space Sandwich Incident that happened one day, during a meteor shower picnic, when young Galaxia accidentally broke her space sandwich. The Giggle Detector sprang into action by declaring a Chuckle Alert! "Zara's sandwich just cracked!" it announced. Zara blushed. "Oops, sorry!" The Giggle Detector winked. "No worries, dear. We'll fix it with extra laughter." And just like that, it went into the Giggle Repair Mode. The Giggle Detector swirled around the broken sandwich. Its nanobots hummed like cosmic bees. "Tickle the crumbs," Professor Quirk advised. Zara giggled, and the sandwich mysteriously mended itself. "Better than new!" she exclaimed.

Yes, laughter is more than just medicine; it's the cosmic glue that holds galaxies together! So, go ahead, giggle, chuckle, and snort, because in Zog, laughter, like a sprinkle of stardust, can fix even a broken space sandwich!

CHAPTER TWENTY-ONE

Dubal's Daring Adventure: The Return to Earth

Once upon a time, in a quiet little town on Earth, a young boy named Dubal embarked on an adventure that was truly out of this world. He journeyed to the far-off planet of Zog with his best friend, an Aliboy named Xain, and experienced wonders beyond his wildest dreams. But as all good things must come to an end, so did Dubal's adventure. With a heavy heart, he bid farewell to Xain and returned to Earth. Upon his return, Dubal was bursting with stories of his time on Zog; telling everyone about crystal mountains that sparkled under the golden suns, of glowing oceans that hummed a soothing melody, and of Zogians who could transform a single tool into anything they desired. His tales were filled with such vivid detail and infectious enthusiasm that everyone in his town was captivated. News of Dubal's extraordinary adventure spread like wildfire. From the bustling cities to the quiet countryside, everyone was talking about Zog. There was a massive scramble to visit this fascinating planet. Its advanced technology intrigued scientists, entrepreneurs saw business opportunities, and ordinary folks dreamed of sightseeing in a land that was straight out of a science fiction novel. Thus, as word spread about Dubal's intergalactic escapade, curiosity swept across the globe. Everyone wanted to hear about Zog, the alien planet with its unique culture and advanced technology. Dubal found himself recounting his experiences, painting vivid pictures of Zog with his words, and that became a job for him as people would literally pay him just to hear captivating tales. But there was one problem. Zog was multiple light-years away. Even with the fastest spaceships, it would take humans many years of nonstop flight to reach Zog. But where there's a will, there's a way. Inspired by Dubal's stories of the Alitool, Earth's brightest minds came together to create their own version of this remarkable device. To help them achieve this, they carefully studied the Alitool spacecraft that Dubal used in his return to Earth, and afterwards, they began to build a replica that relied on nuclear fuel instead of cosmic gas. After months of hard work and countless trials, they finally succeeded; The Earthly Alitool was now a reality, and just like the original, this one was a technological marvel. It could bend space and time, creating a wormhole that allowed instant travel to Zog.

With this invention, the dream of visiting Zog was no longer a distant reality but a tangible possibility. Also, the human Alitool, much like the Zogian one, could transform into anything. But it had an additional feature. It could create a shortcut through space, which could take humans to Zog in no time.

With the Alitool, travelling to Zog became as easy as taking a stroll in the park. And soon, millions descended on Zog. Some came to sightsee, to witness the crystal mountains and the glowing oceans.

Others came seeking business opportunities, eager to trade with the Zogians, and the rest were there just to learn from its advanced technology. Zog was buzzing with activity, its once tranquil atmosphere now filled with the excited chatter of Earthlings. Some of the new arrivals were also busy setting up intergalactic trade and exchange deals. The Zogians, unused to tourists, warmly welcomed the Earthlings, happy to share their world and also to gain knowledge about Earth. The Earthlings, in turn, were respectful visitors. They admired the Zogian way of life, their simple living, and their sustainable practices.

But the massive influx of visitors had a profound impact on the planet. Before long, the Zogians, with their simple and sustainable lifestyle, became overwhelmed. But being the hospitable beings they were, they welcomed the Earthlings with open arms and continued to share their knowledge of the Alitool, showed them the wonders of their planet, and even participated in friendly games of Galactic Goulash and Stellar crust. The journey was not just a physical expedition, but a journey of learning and understanding. The Earthlings learned about a different way of life, one that was in harmony with nature and focused on sustainability. They saw how the Zogians used their Alitools to meet their needs without depleting their planet's resources. This was a stark contrast to Earth, where resources were rapidly dwindling due to overconsumption and mismanagement.

The Earthlings returned home with not just souvenirs, but also valuable lessons. They realised the importance of living sustainably and started implementing changes. They used the knowledge gained from the Alitool to develop more efficient and eco-friendly technologies. The journey to Zog had a ripple effect, leading to a global shift towards sustainability. In the end, Dubal's adventure to Zog turned out to be more than just a thrilling escapade. It was a catalyst for change, a beacon of hope, and a testament to the power of friendship and understanding. And as Dubal gazed at the starry sky each night, he thought about

Xain; then he felt proud for being the one who started the Earthlings in a sustainable direction.

CHAPTER TWENTY-TWO

The Grand Human Arrival on Planet Zog: A Tale of Intergalactic Adaptation and Order

At a time when the asteroid orchestra played melodies of the universe, an event of monumental proportions unfolded. A multitude of humans, those intriguing beings from Earth with their dexterous thumbs and fondness for capturing their own images, descended upon Zog like a shower of talcum dust at a celestial celebration. Their arrival was as unforeseen as a meteor shower, interrupting a quiet afternoon tea. But what ensued? Ah, my dear young Zoglings, that's where our epic narrative takes a wicked turn. You see, the Zogians, with their triad of eyes, stared in astonishment as the humans arrived, bringing with them characteristics unique to Earth: an insatiable curiosity, a tendency towards disorder, and an inexplicable affection for socks of differing patterns. The atmosphere in Zog was charged with anticipation. The authorities were on edge, their antennae quivering with nervous excitement as they eagerly awaited what the future held. How were they to handle this sudden surge of two-legged visitors?

The humans had a peculiar habit. They laughed. Profusely at times. Their laughter reverberated across Zog's iridescent hills, causing annoying ripples in the atmosphere. "We require a Giggle Gauge!" proclaimed one Alichief, his voice echoing through the council chamber. "A device to monitor humour and avert cosmic chortles."

And as if that wasn't bad enough, there was also the Interstellar Sandwich Saga because the humans had a knack for disassembling space sandwiches and causing crumbs to scatter in the zero-gravity environment, floating like miniature asteroids. That was a massive environmental problem for the Council authorities. "We must establish Sandwich Restoration Brigades!" the Alimayor announced, her voice filled with determination. "Every sandwich deserves to remain whole to allow our miniature Alitools to float freely!"

Then there was the Visa Predicament. The humans thronged Zog's interstellar ports with no tickets, visas, or official documents. "We need visas!" Alicaptain Quill roared, his voice echoing through the bustling port. "Cosmic passports, if you will. Only those with the highest giggle quotient shall gain free entry."

With things going from bad to worse on Zog because of what the Zogians regarded as the human infestation, the authorities knew they had to act, and fast! This led to the Formation of Zog's Constabulary, made up of The Stellar Constables. These underwent rigorous training. They donned badges shaped like stars and wielded feather dusters as symbols of their authority. "Maintain the peace," Sergeant Sparkle instructed his new recruits. "Ensure no one, not even a comet, crosses the line!"

With the Stellar Constabulary now in place, the newly commissioned officers went ahead to create The Galactic Visa Bureau. The human arrivals formed orderly queues, forms clutched in their hands. "Visa or no entry!" Officer Luna declared; her voice firm yet fair. "But I'm merely a tourist!" protested young Timmy from Dublin in Ireland, a mere seventeen Earth years old. "I simply wish to ride a meteor, and then I'll be gone! You won't even know I was here." But the visa officer wasn't buying his argument. "Let me repeat myself in case I wasn't clear enough the last time. Visa or no entry!"

And thus, life on Zog gradually returned to its pre-human tranquillity. The Giggle Gauge hummed contentedly, space sandwiches remained intact, and the Zogians resumed their picnics under the gold dust. As the old Zogian saying goes: "When chaos descends, sprinkle it with giggles."

And that, my little interstellar explorers, is the tale of how Zog regained its sparkle by controlling the human presence.

CHAPTER TWENTY-THREE

A Cosmic Language: Words Used on Zog

Aliboy: This is a term for a boy alien. Imagine you're playing a game of intergalactic football, and you need a term for your extraterrestrial teammate. You could say, "Pass the ball, Aliboy!" It's a fun way to add a cosmic twist to your games. Or, Imagine you're playing a game of intergalactic explorers with your friends. You could be an Aliboy, a young alien from the far-off planet of Zog. Use it in a sentence like, "As an Aliboy, I have the power to travel through galaxies!" So, next time you're playing pretend and you're an alien, remember, you're an Aliboy!

Aligirl: This refers to a girl on Zog. In the same game as the Aliboys,' a girl could be an 'Aligirl,' a brave alien female youngster ready to take on any space adventure. Use it in a sentence like, "Watch out, universe! Here comes the Aligirl!" And suppose you're writing a story about an alien who loves to dance. You could write, "The Aligirl twirled under the stars, her moves as mesmerising as a comet's trail." So, if you're a girl pretending to be an alien, you can proudly tell people you're an Aligirl!

Alimum: This term is for a mother. If you're pretending to be a family of aliens, the mother could be called the Alimum. When you're pretending to be a family of aliens, your mum could be the 'Alimum', the caring alien mother who makes sure all her little aliens are well-fed and ready for their space journey. Use it in a sentence like, "Alimum, what's for dinner tonight? Are we having Zogspaghetti?"

Alidad: You guessed it! Alidad is the term for fathers on Zog. They're just like dads on Earth, but they probably have cooler alien dad jokes! In your make-believe alien world, you could say, "Alidad, can we go on a space adventure today?" Yes, your dad would be the 'Alidad', the wise alien father who guides his family through the cosmos. Use it in sentences like, "Alidad, tell us a story about the stars."

Aliteen: This refers to an alien in their teenage years. Imagine you're creating a comic about teenage aliens. You could have a character called "Aliteen" who's always trying to fit in at their intergalactic school. As a teenager, you can sometimes feel like an alien, so why not embrace it and identify yourself as an Aliteen?

Alitot: This adorable term is used for toddlers on Zog. If you have a little sibling who's acting like a cute little alien, you can call them an Alitot! Picture a tiny alien learning to take its first float in zero gravity. You could say, "Look at that Alitot, floating around like a little asteroid butterfly!"

Alibling: This term has nothing to do with a human superstar called Ali wearing lots of bling; no, this term is for an alien sibling. If you and your sibling are pretending to be aliens, you could refer to each other as Aliblings. For example, "Alibling, let's explore this new planet together!"

Alipal: This is a term for a friend. If you've made a new friend at school, you could say, "You're my Alipal because you're out of this world!" So, if you have a friend who loves aliens as much as you do, they're your Alipal!

Alimate: If you're sharing with someone else, they could be your Alimate; for example, your roommate who shares your space (and your toys!). Use it in a sentence like, "My Alimate snores like a space monster!" Or you could say, "My Alimate keeps leaving their toys in our spaceship!" If you share your classroom, they're not just your friends, they're also your Alimates!

Alivisor: This is a term for an alien supervisor. The next time you play a game where someone is in charge, you could say, "Our Alivisor says it's time to refuel our spaceship." Therefore, your teacher or your boss at your part-time job is the Alivisor, the supervisor who oversees that everything runs without a hitch. Use it in a sentence like, "Our Alivisor gave us a fun project today!"

Alident: As a student, you're an Alident; a student learning about things like the universe, for example. Use it in a sentence like, "As an Alident, I'm always ready to learn new things!". If you're studying for a test, you could say, "I'm an Alident preparing for my intergalactic exams or Zog Leaving Cert Exams."

Alteacher: This refers to an alien teacher; the wise alien who imparts knowledge to learners. Use it in a sentence like, "Our Alteacher taught us about the planets today!" Or, if you're playing school, the person who's the teacher could be referred to as the Alteacher. For example, "Excuse me, Alteacher, please how do you multiply alien numbers?"

Aldriver: This is a term for a vehicle driver. The school bus driver or your dad when he's driving could be the Aldriver, the one who navigates through traffic. Use it in a sentence like, "Our Aldriver got us to school safely today." And in a situation where you're playing with toy cars, you could say, "I'm the Aldriver of this lunar rover."

Alpilot: This refers to an alien pilot. If you're pretending to fly a spaceship, you could say, "As the Alpilot, I'll navigate us through the asteroid belt." Otherwise, when you're steering the spaceship in your game, you're the Alpilot, the one guiding the ship through dangerous asteroids. Use it in a sentence like, "Hold tight, everyone; this is your Alpilot, I'll safely get you to your destination!"

Aliking: The leader of your team could be the Aliking, the ruler of the alien crew. Use it in a sentence like this one, "Our Aliking made a great plan for our mission." And assuming that you plan to play a game where someone takes the role of the king, you could say, "All hail the Aliking of Mars!"

Alienqueen: This is an alien female ruler; for example, you could say, "Long live the Alienqueen of Venus!" So, when the leader is a female, she could be the Alienqueen, the queen of the cosmos.

Alitool: Aliens in Zog only need this single tool to make everything in their world – from their cars to their homes. This means that the tool means everything to all aliens in Zog, because they use it to design, manufacture, operate, and service everything in their world. Now, let's assume that you're playing with building blocks; you could then say, "I wish I had an Alitool to build this space station faster!" In such a game, the Alitool could be a wonder device that can transform into any device or equipment you need. To use this noun in a sentence, you could say, "I used my Alitool to build that fort you see over there!"

INDEX OF DANDY AHURUONYE'S BOOKS 

The Eel, The Duck, and The Groccolli Ring of Love – 2023
Why Did the Wasp Come? – 2023
Roosta & Henn: The Rise of AI Robots – 2023
Lower – 2023
Dodo Returns – 2024
Pet Paradise – 2024
Nightlife Of Mannequins – 2024
HISTORY TREE and The Wrinkles of Time – 2024
Dandy Ahuruonye's Fridge Of Secrets – 2024
The Extraordinary World of Ordinary Objects – 2024
Dandy Ahuruonye's Cheeky Periwinkles – 2024
The Hibernuats: A Tale of Human Hibernation – 2024

THE HUNGRY ALIEN
from
PLANET ZOG

—•—

Dandy Ahaoma
AHURUONYE

Lifetime Stories from The Whispering Poet
dandyahuruonyebooks@gmail.com

Don't miss out!

Visit the website below and you can sign up to receive emails whenever Dandy Ahaoma Ahuruonye publishes a new book. There's no charge and no obligation.

https://books2read.com/r/B-A-PXCIB-KJSDD

BOOKS 2 READ

Connecting independent readers to independent writers.